TERROR ON
CEMETERY
HILL

TERROR ON CEMETERY HILL

A Sarah Capshaw Mystery

Drew Stevenson

COBBLEHILL BOOKS
Dutton   New York

For Gale Nancy,
and ten wonderful, loving years together,
and for Karen and Mark Keller with fond memories of
Christmas Eves past.

Library of Congress Cataloging-in-Publication Data
Stevenson, Drew, date
Terror on Cemetery Hill: a Sarah Capshaw mystery/Drew Stevenson.
p.   cm.
Third Sarah Capshaw mystery.
Summary: Only super detective Sarah Capshaw could link the
Wilsonburg Bank robbery with a monster sighting on Cemetery Hill.
ISBN 0-525-65217-5
[1. Mystery and detective stories.] I. Title.
PZ7.S84725Te 1996 [Fic]—dc20 96-13873 CIP AC

Published in the United States by Cobblehill Books,
an affiliate of Dutton Children's Books,
a division of Penguin Books USA Inc.
375 Hudson Street, New York, New York 10014

Designed by Jean Krulis
Printed in the United States of America
First Edition 10 9 8 7 6 5 4 3 2 1

"You don't believe in monsters, do you?"
—Clark Lannigan

"A good detective has to keep an open mind
about *everything*."
—Sarah Capshaw

1

THE DINNER rush was over and things were quiet at the diner that Thursday night. My best friend, Frog Fenniman, and I were sitting in a booth doing our homework. At least *I* was doing mine. Frog was mostly eating French fries and complaining about all the work our teachers give us.

Another friend, Sarah Capshaw, was sitting at the counter between Mrs. Esterly, our town historian, and Hank Radky, the Chief of Police. Sarah had been talking to Mrs. Esterly about local history, but now turned her attention to Radky who was trying to relax over a cup of coffee.

□

"According to the newspaper, the Village Bandit is heading this way," she declared, waving a copy of the *Pittsburgh Post-Gazette* in the air. "He just hit a bank in Leesville a couple of hundred miles east of here."

Sarah was talking about a lone bank robber who had been in the papers lately. Reporters were calling him the Village Bandit because he specialized in robbing banks in little towns. His crime spree had started way up in New England and he had been heading west, knocking off banks on a regular basis along the way.

"I think the Wilsonburg Bank should be under twenty-four-hour police surveillance," Sarah declared.

Radky just sighed and sipped his coffee.

"Speaking of banks, has anyone seen Paul Carmichael tonight?" Mabel, the waitress, asked, glancing up at the clock over the grill which read 8:20.

Paul Carmichael is a teller at the Wilsonburg Bank. Every Thursday night he and Alfred Pennyman, the bank's president, work late at the bank after it closes.

"Mr. Pennyman always sends him over here at 8:00 to pick up coffee and sandwiches," Mabel said. "He's late tonight."

□

"Mabel has a crush on Paul," Goldie, our other waitress, teased.

"Well, he *is* the best-looking bachelor in town," Mabel laughed. "Too bad I'm old enough to be his mother."

Radky finished his coffee.

"Sarah's got me thinking. Maybe I'll just swing over to the bank and make sure everything is all right."

Sarah jumped up. "I'll go with you. You might need backup."

"I'll call you if I need you," Radky said, heading to the cash register.

As I glanced out the window at the quiet street, a battered black van passed under the streetlight and disappeared.

"Someday the Chief is going to treat me like a colleague," Sarah sighed as she slid into our booth. "Instead of like a . . ."

"Pest," I finished for her.

Radky left and a party of four came in. Mabel dropped menus off at their booth and Goldie brought glasses of water. Fred McGhee, our counterman, put down his horse racing form and hit the grill when Mabel shouted orders to him. The room filled with the sound of burgers frying, dishes clattering, Goldie and Mabel laughing, Dad singing in the

□

kitchen, and the cash register ringing as Mrs. Esterly paid her bill.

I couldn't help grinning. To me, Lannigan's Miracle Diner, which my family owns and operates in beautiful downtown Wilsonburg, Pennsylvania, is the greatest show on earth. Even though Wilsonburg is a small town twenty miles down the Monongahela River from Pittsburgh, the readers of a dining magazine in the city voted our diner the best in the western part of the state. People drive out of their way to eat with us. Like my Dad says, "The joint is usually jumping!"

I saw Dad come out of the kitchen and say something to Mom, who was standing at the cash register. Her eyes and mouth flew open in surprise.

"Come on," I said to Frog and Sarah as Dad returned to the kitchen. "Something's up."

We slipped through the swinging door and found Dad leaning over the police scanner which he keeps next to one of his stoves.

"Chief Radky is on the scanner," he said. "Someone just robbed the Wilsonburg Bank and he's calling the State Police for roadblocks."

2

BEFORE DAD could stop us, we darted from the kitchen and out the front door. Sarah led the way as we ran down Main Street to the next corner where the Wilsonburg Bank is. The front of the bank was dark, but we could see a light deep inside. Sarah tried the door and, to our surprise, it opened.

We stepped into the lobby and walked by the ATM machine to the next door, which was also unlocked. It was strange being inside the bank in the dark. Sarah led us down the row of teller windows to Mr. Pennyman's office at the back where the light was shining and someone was shouting.

□

As we entered the office, I gasped at the scene before us. Mr. Pennyman and Paul Carmichael were sitting on the floor, their hands handcuffed to the iron radiator against the wall. Both men looked rumpled and roughed up in their suits. What little hair Mr. Pennyman has was standing straight up on his head. He was the one doing the shouting.

"This is an outrage! An absolute outrage!"

Chief Radky was standing off to one side talking into his radio. Paul Carmichael was just sitting there looking dazed.

"What happened?" Sarah asked him.

"I left at eight o'clock to get coffee and sandwiches the way I always do," Paul explained. "I had just unlocked the front door and stepped outside when a guy in a ski mask jumped out of the shadows and put a pistol to my head. He said he was the Village Bandit and that if I did what I was told no one would get hurt."

"Go on," Sarah urged.

"He pushed me inside and back to the office. First he handcuffed me to the radiator. Then he . . ."

"Then he forced *me* to open the vault and fill canvas bags with money," Mr. Pennyman shrieked. "After that, he handcuffed me next to Carmichael here and disappeared."

"If Chief Radky hadn't come to check on us and

□

6

found the front door unlocked, we might have been handcuffed here all night," Paul finished.

By then Radky was putting his radio away.

"The State Police are throwing up roadblocks all around the county," he pointed out. "The robber can't have gotten out of the area yet, so there's a chance they'll get him."

"And what about *us*?" Mr. Pennyman demanded angrily.

"I just called the station," Radky said. "A deputy is bringing over a bunch of our handcuff keys. If they don't work, we'll have to cut the cuffs off."

That's when Radky noticed us.

"What are you kids doing in here?" he snapped. "This is a crime scene. Get out and don't touch anything."

Even Sarah knew better than to argue with Radky when he uses that tone of voice.

As we walked back to the diner, I thought about the good old days BEFORE SARAH. For excitement Frog and I used to sit on a hill above the river, counting the barges traveling upstream and downstream. And then last summer Sarah Capshaw, amateur detective, came to town. She lived in Pittsburgh and, like Frog and me, had just finished fifth grade. She was spending the summer with her grandparents, while her parents were out of the

□

country on business. At the end of the summer, and after helping her solve two very scary mysteries, Frog and I expected her to go home. Peace would return to our little town.

Then came the announcement. Frog and I were sitting in the diner when Sarah came in. We thought she wanted to say good-bye. What she wanted to say was *hello*.

"Guess what!" she exclaimed. "My parents have decided to move to Wilsonburg! Now we can solve mysteries together all year long."

My attention was brought back to the present by Frog.

"A bank robbery in Wilsonburg," he sighed. "What next?"

Little did I know then that what was next for us was a lot of terror!

3

As USUAL, the next morning I walked to the diner for breakfast before school. I couldn't help enjoying the cool, crisp air. It had been a great autumn. Here it was almost Halloween, and most of the trees were holding their leaves. The surrounding hills were still putting on a beautiful show of bright colors.

Of course, everybody at the diner was talking about the bank robbery. Mabel declared it the biggest thing to happen in town since little Melvin Lydecker got his head stuck in a sewer pipe and had to be cut out.

□

As I sat at the counter eating a Western omelet, I heard Goldie say that Chief Radky had been in for an early breakfast. He told her that the State Police roadblocks had come up empty. He also said he hadn't been able to lift any fingerprints at the bank.

"He wasn't too surprised about that, though," Goldie explained. "Paul Carmichael said the bank robber was wearing gloves."

By that night, things were quieting down, especially when we heard on the news that the Village Bandit had struck again. Less than twenty-four hours after robbing our bank, he had successfully stuck up a bank in a little town in Ohio. It was obvious he was continuing his crime spree westward and was long gone from our area.

The next morning was Saturday, so Frog met me at the diner for breakfast. We were just digging into pancakes spread with Dad's homemade apple butter when the boy came in.

"Hey," I said. "Isn't that the new kid in town?"

Frog looked up from his stack of cakes and nodded.

"Yeah. His name is Randall Davis. He's in the fifth grade. His Mom is the new caretaker at the cemetery."

The cemetery Frog was talking about is the Wilsonburg Cemetery outside of town. I knew that Randall and his mother had moved here from Pitts-

□

burgh and were now living in the caretaker's house on the cemetery grounds.

I watched as Randall stepped up to my mother at the cash register. Mom listened to what he said, and then led him over to our booth.

"Clark. Frog. This is Randall Davis. He's looking for Sarah," Mom introduced us before returning to her post.

"I heard she comes in here a lot," Randall said.

"*Everybody* comes in here a lot!" I proclaimed proudly as I slid over so he could sit down.

"What's the matter?" Frog asked. "Is your life too happy and peaceful?"

"What do you mean?" Randall wondered.

"What he means is that Sarah Capshaw is a trouble magnet," I explained.

"That's what I heard," Randall said grimly. "And that's why I'm looking for her."

"What?" Frog and I cried together. "Why?"

Randall stared down at the tabletop. For a minute he just sat there.

"Are you OK?" I finally asked.

"I think I better wait and talk with Sarah," he answered.

"She usually meets us here," I explained, "but she hasn't shown up yet."

"Yeah," Frog added. "So you might as well fill us in. Whether we like it or not, we're her assistants."

□

Randall looked at Frog and then at me. I could see he was sizing us up, seeing if we could be trusted. When he made up his mind, his words came out in a rush.

"There's . . . there's something weird going on up on Cemetery Hill. I'm . . . I'm afraid."

"Weird? Cemetery Hill? Afraid?" Frog croaked.

"I've got to go now," Randall said. "Mom has work for me to do this morning. Please tell Sarah I'm looking for her."

With that, he slid out of the booth and hurried away.

4

FROG AND I were finishing our breakfast when Sarah finally showed up. She was carrying a map of the United States, which she unfolded on the table-top.

"By tracking the Village Bandit on this map, I'll eventually be able to predict where he'll strike next," she explained. "Then I'll warn the FBI and they can set up an ambush for him."

"Give it up," I groaned.

"I've circled each of the towns where the Bandit has struck," Sarah went on. "He's been robbing a bank roughly every five hundred miles. According to

□

my calculations, his next robbery will occur some-where in western Indiana. I just haven't figured out exactly what town yet."

"Forget the Village Bandit!" I interrupted. "We may have a case for you right here in Wilsonburg."

As I told her about our strange conversation with Randall Davis, she stopped staring at the map and began staring at me. No sooner had I finished than she practically dragged us outside.

"So tell me about this graveyard," she said as we walked along Route 40 on our way to the cemetery.

"Make no *bones* about it," Frog piped up. "It's a real *dead* end."

He then shrieked with laughter.

"C'mon!" Sarah pleaded. "Work with me here. A good detective doesn't like going into a case com-pletely in the dark if she can help it. A little back-ground never hurts. I already know that Ms. Davis is the new caretaker of the cemetery. And that she and Randall just moved into the caretaker's house. Who was the caretaker before her?"

"That was old Oliver Grimes," I answered. "He was the caretaker for as long as anyone could re-member."

"He died at the beginning of the summer," Frog added.

"It took them a long time to replace him," Sarah commented.

☐

"It's a big job and doesn't pay very much," I said. "Before Ms. Davis came along, only Oliver's nephew, Doug Grimes, and Ben Hardwick had even applied for it. But Mr. Hardwick got a better-paying job somewhere else."

By then we were passing between thick woods lining both sides of the highway. When the trees finally thinned out we could see the Wilsonburg Cemetery up ahead. The cemetery spreads out over a hill and is surrounded by a chain-link fence. We paused at the front gate, which was open for Saturday visitors.

The newer part of the cemetery is spread out around the base of the hill. The gravestones are well cared for, with flowers and flags, and the grounds are kept neat. The older part of the cemetery is on top of the hill beyond a thick grove of pines.

"That's Cemetery Hill up there," I pointed out.

The caretaker's house sits just inside the gate next to the start of the cemetery drive. The house is made out of stone with a rounded tower at one of the corners.

It had been a long time since I had been out that way. I had forgotten just how spooky the caretaker's house looks. Of course, being far from town an[d] surrounded by gravestones doesn't help it either[.]

We walked through the gate and up towa[rd] house. In the distance an attractive woman [?] was raking leaves. It was Randall's mot[her]

□

waved and we waved back. We stepped up to the door. Sarah pressed the doorbell and Randall answered.

"Sarah Capshaw?" he said hopefully.

"At your service," Sarah bowed.

"Thanks for coming," he said as we stepped into the hall.

"I understand you've been looking for me," Sarah said.

Randall just stared down at his sneakers. There was a long silence.

"If I'm going to help you, you've got to tell me what this is all about," Sarah prodded him.

Randall nodded his head, and looked up.

"This is all about the monster I saw up on Cemetery Hill."

5

"MONSTER?" FROG CROAKED.

"Let's talk up in my observatory," Randall suggested.

"Observatory?" I wondered, as we followed him upstairs to the second floor.

Randall led us down a hall that ended in a room in the corner tower.

"This is my bedroom, but I call it the observatory," he explained.

All the furniture in the room was arranged around the curving wall. In the spaces between the windows, Randall had hung charts of the stars and

□

posters of the planets. There were several bookcases filled with books on astronomy. But what first caught my eye as we entered the room was an expensive-looking telescope sitting on a tripod in front of the window facing north.

"Astronomy is my hobby," Randall said.

Sarah plopped down in a swivel chair next to the telescope.

"All right. Let's talk about monsters."

Randall took a deep breath before speaking.

"Last night I took my telescope up on Cemetery Hill. The moon was almost full, and I wanted to study its craters."

"You didn't go up there alone, did you?" Frog gasped.

"Of course I did. I'm not afraid of cemeteries. Or at least I wasn't then.

"I set up the telescope on top of the hill," he went on. "The moon was so bright it was like a streetlight. And then I saw it."

"It?" Frog whispered.

"I saw something moving up the hill around the gravestones. At first I thought it was a man. I was scared because no one is allowed in the cemetery after dark. Then I pointed the telescope at him and got *really* scared. It wasn't a man. It was a monster! And no sooner did I see it than it saw me."

"What did you do?" Frog asked with a shudder.

□

18

"I threw my telescope over my shoulder and didn't stop running until I was safely back here."

"What did this monster look like?" I asked, not sure I wanted to know.

"It was a face you see in nightmares," was all Randall would say.

"Did you tell your mother about this?" Sarah asked.

"No. Who would believe a story like that? Besides, Mom took me to a monster movie in Pittsburgh Thursday night. She'd just say it overstimulated my imagination."

"Sarah?" Randall went on. "Would you go up on Cemetery Hill and investigate? Maybe that monster movie did get to me. Maybe it was all my imagination. That's what I'm hoping."

Sarah swiveled in the chair and stared out the window toward Cemetery Hill. Then she swiveled back.

"I'm currently working on the case of the Village Bandit," she said. "But I think I can fit another case in. We'll come back tonight and check it out for you. If there is a monster on Cemetery Hill, we'll find it."

"I can't come back tonight," Frog piped up. "I have to clip Churchill's toenails."

Churchill is Frog's pet bulldog.

"And I have to help him," I quickly added.

☐

If looks could kill, Sarah's glare would have melted us down on the spot. And if I had known then what was waiting for us up on Cemetery Hill, I would have preferred it!

6

SARAH WAS QUIET as we walked back along the highway to town.

"All right," I finally said. "What's on your mind?"

"I'm just wondering if Randall was telling us the truth," she answered.

"Do you think he might have been lying about the monster?" I said.

"He's new in town and hasn't made any friends yet," Sarah replied. "He may have made up that story, hoping to get some attention."

"Let's hope so," I whispered under my breath.

□

"Uh oh," Frog said when we got back to Main Street. "Look who's coming."

If you didn't live in Wilsonburg, you might think it was a Gypsy fortune-teller. The woman was wearing a long colorful dress, with a flowing robe trailing behind it. Her clothes were covered with glittering stars and strange-looking symbols.

"It's Beatrice Biddle," I pointed out, even though Sarah and Frog knew perfectly well who she was.

Actually everyone in town knows her. She used to work at the Wilsonburg Bank. After retiring, she decided to devote her life to studying the supernatural and proving that it's for real. She was quickly joined by ten friends and they formed the Wilsonburg Searchers for Psychic Truth. The Searchers spend their time holding séances and investigating haunted houses and ghostly sightings. Mrs. Biddle is the group's leader and guiding light.

"I bet she's on her way to the cemetery to try and make contact with the afterlife or something," Sarah suggested.

"No," I replied. "She and the Searchers are banned from the Wilsonburg Cemetery."

I explained how they used to hang around the cemetery, trying to contact the dear departed. They ended up scaring other visitors with their weird behavior. Finally, they were told they couldn't enter

□

the cemetery without a legitimate reason. And supernatural investigations were *not* considered a legitimate reason.

As she came closer, I could see how Mrs. Biddle could scare someone who didn't know her. She's a big woman with a booming voice. And when she thinks she's hot on the trail of a ghost or something, she gets this wild crazy look in her eyes.

Mrs. Biddle had her Psycho-Meter strapped to her head. It looks like a small radar and when she has it turned on, it spins around and around. She claims it helps her detect vibrations from the spirit world.

"Isn't this just the most delicious day?" she cried when she recognized us.

We smiled and nodded.

"All Hallows' Eve is coming," she went on. "Can't you just feel the restlessness in the spirit world?"

We kept smiling and nodding.

"You must excuse me now," she said, sweeping by us in a flurry of perfumed scarves. "I must go home and put fresh batteries in my Psycho-Meter. I'm surely going to be needing it soon."

"Happy ghost hunting!" Frog called after her.

"Better her than us," I thought grimly to myself.

We stopped at the diner for a snack and sat in a

□

booth discussing Randall's weird story.

"You don't believe in monsters, do you?" I nervously asked Sarah.

"A good detective has to keep an open mind about *everything*," she answered.

It wasn't the answer I wanted to hear.

7

We met later that night at the diner. I arrived early and helped Dad in the kitchen. When Sarah and Frog came, I hung up my apron and we headed out of town.

Sarah was wearing her fedora hat over her long blonde hair. She only wears it when she's on a case. She thinks it makes her look like a detective in an old movie.

When we arrived at the cemetery, the front gates were closed and locked, so we had to climb over. Off to the right there were lights on in the care-taker's house. I felt better knowing that Ms. Davis

□

was on the grounds, although the top of Cemetery Hill is a long way away from the house.

All around us, gravestones and mausoleums reflected the ghostly moonlight as we started up the narrow cemetery drive. The road became steeper as it approached the pine grove, which marks the end of the newer part of the cemetery. The tall pines blocked the moonlight, and the night became pitch black as the road cut through them. A breeze started up, and the needles began to rattle like bones. We walked faster.

I was glad when the road finally emerged from the trees. Glad, that is, until I saw the older part of the cemetery. Everything about it is wilder and spookier than down below. The trees are bigger and more gnarled. The grass is longer and the bushes more scraggly. No one has been buried up there in many years, and some of the gravestones are tilting to one side. Others have fallen over completely.

I had heard people talking about Cemetery Hill at the diner. Everyone agrees that the entire cemetery is just too large for one caretaker to manage. But the town can only afford to pay one. Therefore, the caretaker is instructed to keep the newer section of the cemetery neat and tidy. That's where people are buried now. And that's where most of the visitors go. Few people venture to the top of Cemetery Hill anymore.

☐

At the very top of the hill is the old Wilson mausoleum. A mausoleum is a large tomb that looks like a small house. People build mausoleums so family members can be buried together above ground.

The Wilson mausoleum looks like it belongs in a horror movie. It's made out of huge blocks of stone. A row of pillars holds up the roof along the front. At each corner of the roof, grotesque gargoyles are hunched down, surveying the landscape with fierce eyes.

"Let's go up to that big mausoleum," Sarah whispered. "We'll have a good view from up there."

Keeping low to the ground, we made our way to the top of the hill. When we reached the Wilson mausoleum, Sarah walked between the pillars and up to the black iron door. Frog and I held back, afraid to move any closer to the huge tomb looming over us. Suddenly Sarah turned on her flashlight.

"What are you doing?" I hissed.

"This door is open," she answered.

Frog and I flicked on our lights and also aimed them at the heavy door. She was right! It *was* open a crack. I held my breath as Sarah pushed against it. With a terrible creaking sound it swung inward.

Sarah started across the threshold. And then it happened! A figure jumped out of the blackness within and grabbed her. Before she could struggle, she was yanked inside the mausoleum. The figure

☐

then ran out the door, but skidded to a stop when it saw Frog and me, frozen with terror, blocking its path.

For one awful moment, it stood there in the beams of our flashlights. It looked like it had just crawled out of a grave. The face was a skull, but not quite. Bits of dead skin still hung from the pale bone. One eye socket was empty. The other still had an eye in it, but it was bulging like it was ready to pop out. The worst part of the horrible mess was the mouth. It was wide open in a silent scream.

And then the creature charged us!

□

8

FROG AND I dove out of the way as the creature ran between us. Then we dashed into the mausoleum and pushed the door shut behind us.

"Night of the Living Dead!" Frog was gasping as he pushed against the door. "Night of the Living Dead!"

He was referring to a movie that was filmed in the Pittsburgh area about the dead rising up out of the grave to attack the living.

I pointed my light at Sarah, who was just getting up off of the marble floor where the creature had thrown her.

□

"Did you see it?" I demanded. "Randall was telling us the truth. It *was* a face you see in nightmares!"

"I didn't have time to see anything," Sarah admitted.

"Well, Frog and I saw it, and it was *horrible*!"

And then I realized that someone *else* was in the mausoleum with us. A woman was lying on her back in the middle of the floor.

"It's Mrs. Biddle," I gasped.

"The monster got her, and he's going to get us too," Frog wailed from the door.

Sarah and I crouched beside the motionless figure. Mrs. Biddle was wearing her Gypsy fortune-teller outfit. Her Psycho-Meter was strapped around her head.

"She's unconscious but breathing," Sarah said. "We've got to get help for her."

"And for ourselves," Frog cried. "French fries! I *need* French fries!"

Frog thinks all the world's problems can be solved with French fries. Whenever something goes wrong in his life, he heads to the diner for a double order of fries, extra crispy.

Sarah pointed her flashlight around. The mausoleum was one big room with a very high ceiling.

"Where are the . . . you know . . . ?" I started to ask nervously.

□

"Bodies?" Sarah finished for me. "They're buried in vaults in the walls. It's called being interred."

The Wilsons were *interred* inside three of the four walls. Each grave was sealed with a long panel of marble bearing the name, birth date, and death date of the person buried in that spot. The graves were arranged, one on top of the other, from floor to ceiling.

"Boy," I whistled. "There sure are a lot of them in here."

Sarah quickly counted the panels, moving from wall to wall.

"I count forty-two," she said when she was finished. "And look at some of the dates carved in the panels."

I felt a tingle run up my neck. Some of the Wilsons buried in the mausoleum were born back in the eighteenth century! These were the same Wilsons who first settled our town and eventually had it named after them.

"Forget the bodies!" Frog ordered. "Get over here and help me hold the door shut."

He was pressing against the door as if he really had the strength to keep the creature from pushing in if it wanted.

"Creature or no creature, we've got to go get help for Mrs. Biddle," Sarah remarked as we joined him.

"No," Frog whimpered.

□

"Listen," I said, putting my hand on his trembling shoulder. "There's not a creature from the grave alive who can outrun Frog Fenniman when he's scared."

"You're right," he agreed. "Being a coward has its rewards."

"Shhhhhh," Sarah hissed, pressing her ear against the door. "I hear something and it's *not* a creature from the grave."

Now I heard it too. Sirens! And they were getting louder and louder.

We turned our lights off, and Sarah opened the door a crack. Peering out into the night, we saw flashing red and yellow lights bursting out of the pine grove below.

"We're saved!" Frog cried.

"Yeah, but we don't want to have to explain what we're doing up here," Sarah pointed out. "Come on!"

We hurried out the door and ducked into some thick bushes growing next to the mausoleum. Peeking out through the thick branches, we watched an ambulance pull up to the door, followed by a police car.

Chief Radky never looked so good. Little did I know then that I'd be thinking the same thing a week later.

□

TWO MEDICS JUMPED from the ambulance and hurried into the mausoleum. Chief Radky and Randall's mother got out of the police car. Radky went in to help the medics, while Ms. Davis stood at the door.

It only took a minute to secure Mrs. Biddle on a stretcher and wheel her out. The ambulance then sped away down the drive. Chief Radky stepped back into the mausoleum. For a few minutes the beam from his flashlight bounced around inside.

"He's investigating the scene," Sarah whispered.

□

Radky stepped outside and pointed his light at the mausoleum door.

"That's how they got in," he remarked. "They broke the lock."

"I'm afraid these old mausoleum locks are rusted and brittle," Ms. Davis pointed out. "And this is the *oldest* mausoleum in the cemetery.

"And what did you mean when you said *they?*" she added.

"Where Beatrice goes, her Searchers follow," Radky explained. "I doubt very much she was alone up here tonight."

"What do you think happened to her in there?"

"It's my guess Beatrice somehow slipped on the marble floor and knocked herself out. The other Searchers then ran out of the cemetery and called 911."

"That would explain why the call was made *anonymously*," Ms. Davis reasoned. "Her friends didn't want to get in trouble too."

Radky shook his head sadly.

"Now I'm going to have to charge Beatrice with trespassing *and* with breaking and entering. She's a dear, sweet soul and wouldn't hurt a fly, but she and her friends have to learn they can't break the law like this."

"I'll get a locksmith up here first thing in the

morning," Ms. Davis said as they walked to the squad car. "And I'll make sure he puts on the biggest, strongest lock he can. No one will ever break in there again without dynamite."

"And if you'll leave the cemetery gate unlocked, I'll have my deputy add the hill to her patrol tonight," Radky said as he held the car door open for Ms. Davis. "I don't think any Searchers would dare come back after what happened, but you never know."

We emerged from the bushes and stared after the squad car as it disappeared into the pine grove.

"I wish we were with them," Frog sighed wistfully. "No creature from the grave is going to mess with Chief Radky."

"And speaking of that," Sarah said, "describe your creature for me."

I did, shuddering the whole time.

"Are you *sure* it wasn't someone wearing a scary mask?" she asked.

"That was no mask!" I insisted. "It was real!"

"Yeah!" Frog added.

"OK," Sarah shrugged. "Let's go get Frog his French fries."

"Wait," Frog said fearfully. "The creature might be out there some place waiting for us."

"Don't worry," I said, trying to reassure *both* of us.

□

"With all the commotion up here tonight, that creature has long since gone back into whatever grave it crawled out of."

"I'm afraid you're right," Sarah agreed as we started down the hill. "There's no chance of another monster sighting tonight."

She sounded disappointed. She was the only one!

10

THE NEXT DAY was Sunday, and Sundays during football season are extra fun at the diner. Mom and Dad are big Pittsburgh Steelers fans. They have two television sets mounted over the grill, so everybody can see. Dad also has a set in the kitchen, which he watches while he cooks. Things sometimes get real rowdy.

I arrived at the diner shortly before the opening kickoff. As usual, we were doing a brisk Sunday business. Randall and his mother were sitting at the

☐

counter finishing their lunches. Ms. Davis was talking with Paul Carmichael, the bank teller, who was sitting next to her.

"It was nice meeting you, Paul," Ms. Davis said as Goldie handed her the check.

"Thank you, but the pleasure was all mine," Paul smiled, taking the check out of her hand. "Please, allow me."

"Thanks, but that's not necessary," Ms. Davis protested.

"Of course it's not *necessary*," Paul answered smoothly. "But it would make me happy to treat. And I can use a little happiness right about now."

As Ms. Davis went to the cash register with Paul, Randall walked over to me.

"What really happened on Cemetery Hill last night?" he asked. "All I know is what Mom told me."

I quickly filled him in on our terrifying encounter.

"So you and Frog saw the creature too?" He whistled when I finished.

"Yeah," I answered. "You're not going crazy."

I could tell he didn't know whether to be relieved or not.

After he and his mother had gone, Sarah and Frog arrived. Paul was still standing at the cash register talking to Mom.

□

"She sure is nice," he was saying about Ms. Davis as we joined him.

"She's also pretty, divorced, and not seeing anyone at the present time," Goldie commented as she hurried by with a tray of steaming food.

"You heard it from the Lannigan Miracle's own gossip columnist," I laughed.

"How are you feeling, Paul?" Sarah asked.

"Still shaken," he admitted.

"It was a terrible, terrible thing," Mom agreed.

Paul nodded. "I've been leaving the bank for coffee and sandwiches just about every Thursday night for two years, and never thought a thing about it. This is Wilsonburg, not some big city."

We nodded our head in sympathy.

"If only I had been more careful, this might not have happened," he finished sadly. "I read the newspapers. I knew the Village Bandit might be heading our way."

"You can't blame yourself," Mom said.

After Paul left, we asked Mom what the news was on Mrs. Biddle.

"She's in the hospital with a concussion," Mom answered. "She's doing well and is seeing visitors."

"In that case, we'll go see her," Sarah said.

"Yeah," I agreed. "But we'll go *after* the Steelers game."

□

We sat at the counter and cheered the Steelers on. Being surrounded by friendly faces and all the usual diner bustle made the cemetery seem far away. But I knew it wasn't far away. And neither was the evil lurking on Cemetery Hill.

□

11

AFTER THE FINAL WHISTLE announced the Steelers victory, Sarah, Frog, and I walked down to the Wilsonburg hospital. We arrived just as Sarah's grandfather was leaving. Conrad Capshaw is a well-known lawyer in western Pennsylvania.

"They're not going to put Mrs. Biddle in jail, are they?" Frog fretted.

"Of course not," Mr. Capshaw answered. "But Beatrice isn't helping her cause by insisting that none of her Searchers were with her, and that some kind of cemetery monster knocked her out."

After Mr. Capshaw left, we stepped quietly into

□

Mrs. Biddle's room. She was lying on the bed, wearing a plain hospital gown, with a bandage wrapped around her head instead of the Psycho-Meter.

"More visitors!" she exclaimed. "How nice!"

Sarah asked if she would tell us how she came to be found unconscious on the floor of the Wilson mausoleum.

"I'm sorry, but Conrad has advised me not to discuss it," she replied. "I'm in trouble, you know."

"Clark and Frog saw the same monster," Sarah prodded.

Mrs. Biddle grinned. "I know they did."

"What?" I cried in amazement.

"One of my Searchers was having lunch at the diner yesterday," Mrs. Biddle explained. "He overheard you talking about it and hurried over to my house and told me."

"We *have* to be more careful," Sarah muttered.

"I know I'm not allowed in the cemetery," Mrs. Biddle admitted. "But I just couldn't resist the chance to encounter a creature from the grave."

"Did any of your Searchers go with you?" Sarah asked.

"No," Mrs. Biddle answered firmly. "I knew if I was going to be breaking the law I had to do so alone."

"What happened to you in the cemetery?" Sarah went on.

□

"At first I just wandered back and forth up Cemetery Hill. My Psycho-Meter was spinning like crazy. The whole area was a hotbed of psychic activity! When I got to the Wilson mausoleum, I noticed that the door was open a crack."

"Are you *sure*?" Sarah asked.

"I would *never* break in!" Mrs. Biddle insisted.

"We believe you," Sarah said. "Please go on."

"I stepped inside, but didn't turn on my flashlight. Creatures from the grave are shy of light, you know. I waited in the darkness and then a figure appeared in the doorway. I turned on my light and saw that it was the creature."

"Weren't you scared?" I gasped.

"Scared *and* excited," Mrs. Biddle admitted. "The face *was* terrible to behold, but I forced myself to approach it."

"You walked toward that . . . that thing!" Frog gasped.

"I am a dedicated searcher for psychic truth," Mrs. Biddle replied solemnly. "As I got closer, I chanted, 'Being from the grave, do not attack, for I am here to welcome you back.' "

"Then what happened?" Frog asked breathlessly.

"At first it seemed unsure of what to do. But then I reached out to it, and it suddenly pushed me away. I fell backward and hit my head on the floor. That's the last thing I remember until I woke up here."

□

43

"Could it have been someone wearing a mask?" Sarah asked.

"That was *no* mask!" Mrs. Biddle declared.

Just then a nurse came in and shooed us out, so Mrs. Biddle could rest.

"That's four of us who have seen the creature," Frog pointed out as we left the hospital. "Randall, Clark, Mrs. Biddle, and me."

"I think we have enough evidence to go to Chief Radky with the truth," I added.

"What evidence?" Sarah cried. "What truth? No one is ever going to believe that three kids saw a monster in a cemetery. And no one *ever* believes Mrs. Biddle."

"In other words, our investigation continues," I said.

"Our investigation continues," Sarah nodded grimly.

□

12

THE NEXT DAY after school, Frog and I stopped at the diner for a snack. While we ate we talked about Halloween, which was coming up the following Saturday.

"Do you have a costume for the party yet?" Frog asked me.

He was talking about the party the Wilsonburg Bank throws every Halloween night at the Community Center.

"Not yet," I admitted. "Do you?"

"Yeah, but it's a secret," he said mysteriously as Sarah joined us.

□

"I just heard on the radio that the Village Bandit robbed a bank in a little town in western Indiana this morning," she told us smugly. "*Just* as *I* predicted."

"Yeah," I quickly pointed out. "But you never predicted exactly *which* town."

Sarah ignored me as she unfolded her map of the United States, and pinpointed the recently victimized Indiana town. First, she circled it with a marker. Then she took a ruler out of her knapsack.

"What are you doing?" Frog asked.

"Obviously, I'm figuring out where the Bandit will strike next. Like I said before, he's been robbing a bank every five hundred miles or so on his way west. With the exception of our bank, that's been his M.O."

"What's a *mo*?" I asked.

"Moe is one of the Three Stooges," Frog pointed out.

"Not mo!" Sarah cried. "*M.O.* It stands for modus operandi."

"The Village Bandit is an opera singer?" Frog wondered.

"Modus operandi has nothing to do with opera!" Sarah howled. "It means method of operation. Criminals often have a certain pattern they follow. The key to a criminal investigation is to discover

□

what that pattern is, and then trap the bad guy at the next crime scene. That's what I'm trying to do with the Village Bandit."

Muttering to herself about Frog and me being the *Two* Stooges, Sarah placed the end of the ruler on the Indiana town that was the scene of the Bandit's last robbery. Then she measured five hundred miles west.

"According to my calculations, the Bandit will strike next at a bank in a small town somewhere in central Iowa," she announced.

"Yeah," I said. "But *which* one? Look, there are a lot of small towns in that part of the state. You don't know which ones even *have* a bank."

"I know, I know," Sarah admitted. "I still have work to do on this."

That's when Mom came in.

"I just came from visiting Beatrice at the hospital," she told everyone.

"How's she doing?" Mabel asked.

"She was sitting up in bed playing with her Ouija board," Mom laughed. "And she asked me to send over a slice of pumpkin pie, so I guess she's feeling better."

"I'll drop the pie off to her on my way home," Sarah volunteered.

Mom went behind the counter and wrapped up

□

the pie. Then she answered the phone, which was ringing behind the cash register. After she hung up, she walked over to our booth.

"That was Randall's mother," she said, handing the pie to Sarah. "She was calling to invite you kids to stay over with him Friday night. She has a date and doesn't want him to be alone."

"Spend the night in the cemetery?" I exclaimed. "No thank you!"

"No way!" Frog cried.

"Cool!" Sarah grinned. "We accept!"

13

THE NEXT MORNING on our way to school, Sarah told us which town would be the Village Bandit's next target.

"Tice Center, Iowa," she declared.

"How did you figure that out?" I wondered.

"Never mind," she replied mysteriously. "A good detective shouldn't give away all her secrets."

"Did you call and tell the FBI?" Frog asked.

"No, I didn't!" she snapped, in a tone of voice that warned Frog and me not to ask anymore questions.

When we stopped at the diner after school that

□ ·

afternoon everyone was talking about the Bandit.

"They finally caught him," Mabel informed us. "He stuck up a bank in Iowa, but this time he didn't get away. The Iowa State Police arrested him after a high-speed car chase."

"What was the name of the town?" I asked.

"Let's see. I think it was called Tice something or other."

"Tice Center!" Frog cried. "Sarah, you were right!"

"As usual," I admitted.

I expected Sarah to brag nonstop about her correct prediction, but she was strangely quiet about it. I was grateful for that.

Usually I look forward to Friday night and the coming weekend. Not that week. Being alone in the cemetery while Ms. Davis was out on her date was bad enough. Sleeping over was something else!

And so on Friday night we were standing in the front hall of the caretaker's house with Randall. No sooner did we lower our overnight bags to the floor than Paul Carmichael arrived.

I grinned. "So you're Ms. Davis's date?"

"Mom will be down in a minute," Randall said.

We left Paul and followed Randall upstairs. Sarah got her own bedroom, but Frog and I had to bunk together. Randall and his mother helped us get settled, and then we all went downstairs.

☐

"There's plenty of food in the kitchen," Ms. Davis said as Paul helped her on with her coat. "And the number of the theater we'll be at is written on the pad next to the phone."

"And speaking of food," Paul added. "After the movie we'll be stopping at the diner for a snack."

"Of course," I beamed.

Ms. Davis paused at the door.

"Are you sure you kids are going to be all right?"

"Aw, Mom!" Randall groaned.

"Sorry," Ms. Davis smiled. "I guess that crazy Biddle woman and her friends won't be coming around anymore."

"Right," Randall agreed. "And with that new lock the locksmith put on the Wilson mausoleum, no one is going to get in there without the key. Everything's fine."

After they left, Sarah opened a door off of the hall.

"What's in here?" she asked, turning on the light and stepping inside.

"That's the cemetery office," Randall explained. "There's a file on every person or family buried here. Genealogists sometimes come by to trace their family roots."

Two walls of the office were lined with file cabinets. Attached to the third wall was a giant map of the cemetery, with each grave and mausoleum

□

marked on it. Next to it was a square of pegboard hung with keys to the mausoleums. In the middle of the room was a desk and a copier.

"Mom gave me money to rent videos," Randall finally said. "Let's go down to Hughey's Video Store."

"You guys go ahead," Sarah said. "I want to look for the file on the Wilson mausoleum. That's the one your monster was entering when he surprised Mrs. Biddle."

I couldn't believe she was going to stay in that spooky house alone, but I knew better than to argue with her.

Randall, Frog, and I walked into town. We were just passing the big house where the Lydeckers live when something jumped out of the bushes and shrieked at us.

My mouth opened so wide I could have swallowed a whole club sandwich in one gulp. Standing before us, in the eerie glow of the streetlight, was the creature from the cemetery!

14

MY HORROR TURNED quickly to amazement. The awful face wasn't *exactly* the same, but close. *Both* eye sockets had bulging eyes in them and the mouth was open in a grin, not a scream. And this creature was only three feet tall and carrying a bag!

"Trick or treat!" the creature shrieked.

"It's just a little kid wearing a monster mask," Randall said with a loud sigh of relief.

The mask was so big it hung down over the kid's shoulders, making him look like a giant head. Since we were standing in front of the Lydecker's house

□

and they have a five-year-old son, it didn't take a Sarah Capshaw to figure out who it was.

"Is that you, Melvin?" Frog cried angrily.

"Trick or treat!" little Melvin Lydecker demanded as he held the bag out to us.

"Forget it!" Frog snapped. "It's not Halloween yet."

"Where did you get that mask, Melvin?" I asked.

"Trick or treat!" Melvin yelled, stamping his foot.

"Does anybody have any candy?" I asked.

We all rummaged in our pockets. No candy, but Frog pulled out a quarter and dropped it in the bag.

"I want a dollar!" Melvin insisted.

"Give him a dollar," I told Frog.

Frog reluctantly put a dollar in the bag.

"All right," I said gently. "Where did you get the mask?"

"It's Dad's," Melvin answered, pulling it off.

"Can I see it?" I went on.

"Give me another dollar," Melvin replied.

Muttering to himself, Frog forked over another buck. As Melvin handed me the mask, I noticed the price tag and label were still attached to the back. I glanced at the label.

"It says this mask is part of the Gruesome Creatures from the Grave series. I guess what we saw on Cemetery Hill was someone wearing another mask from this series."

□

54

I was relieved and angry. Relieved that there was no monster. Angry that someone had fooled us.

"Where did your dad buy this?" I asked Melvin.

"At a store in Pittsburgh," Melvin answered. "He's going to wear it when he takes me to the Halloween party."

With that he grabbed the mask out of my hand and trotted up the yard toward his house.

"That kid has always been more trick than treat," Frog grumbled.

"I can't believe the creature was really just someone wearing a mask," I said as we continued on to the video store. "It looked so *real* up on Cemetery Hill."

"We shouldn't feel too bad," Frog pointed out. "Mrs. Biddle was fooled too."

"But who was behind the mask?" Randall wondered. "And why did they want to scare us?"

We had no answer for that.

We got our videos and hurried back to the cemetery. Sarah was sitting at the desk in the office surrounded by papers.

I told her about Melvin Lydecker and the mask. By the time I finished she was laughing.

"You never did believe there was a real monster on Cemetery Hill, did you?" Frog accused her.

"Let's just say I had *grave* doubts," Sarah grinned.

□

15

SARAH?" RANDALL ASKED. "Who do *you* think was behind that monster mask on Cemetery Hill?"

"Maybe someone who wanted the caretaker's job, but didn't get it," Sarah reasoned. "Didn't two men apply for the job before Ms. Davis? You said one of them got a better job elsewhere. What about the other one? Didn't you say he was the old caretaker's nephew?"

"Doug Grimes," I nodded. "But no one would *ever* hire him for anything."

"Yeah," Frog agreed. "He's is *in* jail more than he's out."

□

"I found this in a desk drawer," Sarah said, handing me a photograph.

The photo showed two men standing in front of the caretaker's house. One was an old man wearing overalls. That was Oliver Grimes, the former caretaker. The picture must have been taken shortly before his death at the beginning of the summer.

"Is the young man this Doug Grimes?" Sarah asked.

I looked at the bald head, the deep-set glaring eyes, the smile that was really a sneer, and nodded.

"That's dear sweet Doug Grimes all right."

"I bet this Doug character wants to scare Mom and me away, so he'll get another chance at the caretaker's job!" Randall cried angrily.

"And Doug is definitely the type to do something rotten like that," I added.

"It wouldn't hurt to find out what Mr. Grimes has been up to lately," Sarah replied.

"That may not be so easy," Frog pointed out. "When he didn't get the job here, he moved to Pittsburgh. I haven't seen him around lately."

"We can ask at the diner," I suggested. "Someone there may know something."

"Good idea," Sarah agreed. "Now look at this."

She handed me one of the sheets of paper spread out on the desk in front of her. It was a diagram of the inside of the Wilson mausoleum, showing which

□

Wilson was buried in which grave. Next to each name was a birth and death date, as well as a grave number.

I shrugged my shoulders. "So?"

"That's the *official* cemetery record for the Wilson mausoleum," Sarah pointed out. "How many people does it say are buried inside?"

I looked at the last name and number on the sheet.

"Forty-one. So?"

"So how many graves did I count that night we were inside the mausoleum with Mrs. Biddle?"

"I don't remember," I admitted.

"Well, I do," Sarah replied. "I counted forty-two marble panels with forty-two names engraved on them. One *more* grave than is listed in the official record."

"What does that mean?" I wondered.

"I don't know," Sarah said, as she replaced the folder in a file cabinet. "Maybe nothing, maybe everything."

After turning off the office light and shutting the door again, we went into the living room and watched our videos. We were just finishing the last one when Ms. Davis came in.

"I had a wonderful time with Paul!" she exclaimed.

"How was the food at the diner?" I asked.

□

58

"Great! I can't wait to have the Hungarian goulash again."

"My dad calls himself the Prince of Paprika," I laughed.

"Sounds like you really like Paul," Randall teased. "Are you going out with him again?"

"As a matter of fact, he invited me to help him chaperon the Community Center Halloween party," Ms. Davis answered. "The bank sponsors it."

She went upstairs and we finished our movie. Then we had another snack and turned in.

Later, I had a terrible nightmare. I dreamed that all the Wilsons buried in the mausoleum left their graves and surrounded the caretaker's house. I woke up in a sweat and vowed I would never again sleep over in a cemetery.

□

16

THE NEXT MORNING Ms. Davis put out a big breakfast for us. Then we helped her rake leaves before
heading back to town.

The day was clear and beautiful. When we
reached the woods along the highway, however, a
shower of crisp leaves swirled down around our
heads, again reminding us that it was Halloween
and fall was coming to an end.

"Let's walk home through the woods," Frog suggested. "We can take the old road."

He was referring to an abandoned road, which

meanders back to town through the woods. It's so rutted and overgrown it hardly even looks like a road anymore. I remember Goldie once saying that when she was in high school kids used the road for a lovers' lane. That was a long time ago.

We turned left where the old road meets the highway. Ten minutes into the woods, we came to a banged-up black van tucked into the trees off to the side.

"That's a strange place to park," Sarah said.

"It probably belongs to a hunter," I suggested.

"I doubt it," Sarah replied. "Look at the thick layer of leaves on it. I'd say it's been here awhile."

"Maybe it's abandoned," Frog said.

Sarah shook her head. "People who abandon vehicles don't leave the license plates on."

"Whoever owns it must be a dog lover," I said, pointing at the license plate. All it had on it was D O G.

Sarah went around peering in all the windows.

"Nothing inside except a police scanner," she pointed out.

"Let's go," I said impatiently. "This is none of our business."

"Yeah," Frog agreed, looking around nervously. "The owner might come along and catch you."

We left the van behind and continued our walk. It

□

took us a lot longer to get back to town than if we had followed the highway, but it was worth it. The woods were really pretty that day.

We each went home to drop off our overnight bags. Then we met at the diner for hot chocolate.

"I was just wondering," Sarah asked in a loud voice, after we had settled into a booth. "Does anyone know what Doug Grimes has been up to lately?"

"No, thank goodness!" Goldie exclaimed.

"He's probably in jail somewhere," Big Walt the truck driver added.

Those were the *nicest* comments anybody around us made about Doug.

I sipped my chocolate and stared out the window at the Saturday traffic on Main Street. And then it hit me! We had been sitting in this same booth the night of the bank robbery. And I had looked out at the street just before Chief Radky left to check on Mr. Pennyman and Paul.

"You know something?" I said, snapping my fingers. "I think I've seen that van before."

Sarah lowered her mug as I explained I had seen it driving up Main Street the night the Wilsonburg Bank was robbed.

"And I bet our bank robber was behind the wheel!" she exclaimed. "That van in the woods was equipped with a police scanner. The robber must

□

have been driving out Route 40 when he heard on the scanner that a State Police roadblock was being set up ahead. So he had to ditch the van and take off on foot."

"How can that be?" I wondered. "If the Village Bandit left his van in the woods, how did he manage to get all the way to Ohio where he robbed that bank the next day?"

"Yeah," Frog agreed. "And you said the van was empty. He couldn't have gotten far lugging those bags of money."

"Obviously it *wasn't* the Village Bandit who robbed our bank," Sarah replied.

"What?" Frog and I cried.

"Think about the Bandit's M.O.," Sarah urged.

"Moe?" Frog wondered.

"Don't start that again!" Sarah warned as she scooped a marshmallow out of her hot chocolate and bounced it off of Frog's forehead.

□

17

"IF THE VILLAGE BANDIT'S modus operandi was to rob banks in places roughly five hundred miles apart, he wouldn't have bothered with the Wilsonburg Bank," Sarah explained.

"Are you saying the Village Bandit *didn't* rob our bank?" I cried in surprise.

"Look at the facts," Sarah urged. "He pulled a robbery a couple of hundred miles east of here in Leesville."

"Yeah," Frog added. "And then he robbed that bank in Ohio a couple of hundred miles west of here."

□

"Exactly," Sarah replied. "So it didn't fit his M.O. to rob our bank in the middle.

"And I'll tell you what else has been bothering me about this case. The Village Bandit wouldn't know that Paul Carmichael leaves the bank every Thursday night at 8:00 to go to the diner to pick up sandwiches. He wouldn't know to be hiding outside the door at that exact moment."

"Only someone who's been around Wilsonburg for awhile would know that," I agreed.

"Could all the weird stuff that's been going on around here be connected?" Sarah wondered. "From the bank robbery to the van in the woods to the terror on Cemetery Hill?"

"It's like connecting dots to make a picture," Frog pointed out. "How are we going to connect *our* dots?"

"First we find out if Doug Grimes's middle name starts with an O," Sarah said.

Before I could ask her what that had to do with anything, she went over and talked with Goldie. When she returned she was grinning.

"Goldie says Doug's full name is Douglas Oliver Grimes. He was named for his uncle, Oliver Grimes, the old cemetery caretaker."

Sarah took her jacket down from the booth's coat tree.

"And now I'm going to the Historical Society and

□

try to find out why there's one more grave in the Wilson mausoleum than appears on the official cemetery record."

She took off, leaving Frog and me speechless. Frog then went home to get his costume ready. I spent the rest of the afternoon helping Dad in the kitchen.

As the light outside began to fade and party time approached, I knew I had to do something about a costume. Since I was wearing an apron and one of Dad's chef hats, I decided I was already in costume.

As I returned to the dining room, a large group was pouring through the door. I was surprised to see that it was Mrs. Biddle with all her Searchers for Psychic Truth. Mrs. Biddle was still wearing her head bandage, but she had fastened her Psycho-Meter on around it.

"I guess Mrs. Biddle is feeling better," I said to Mom.

"It would take more than a concussion to keep Beatrice in on Halloween night," Mom replied with a grin.

Frog arrived shortly after. He was dressed like a robo-cop. His clothes were wrapped in aluminum foil. He had a tool belt around his waist with some kind of plastic laser gun tucked inside it. The weird-est part of the getup was the top of his head. He had strapped on a red emergency light. Standing in the

□

middle of the room, he turned it on. Everyone applauded as the light began to spin around and around.

"How do you like my chef's costume?" I asked him hopefully.

I could tell he didn't think much of it. And then Sarah arrived, wearing a trench coat and her hat.

"Nice costume, Frog," she said. "Dumb costume, Lannigan."

"Well, at least it's more original than dressing up like a detective," I snapped.

"Randall is waiting for us at the cemetery," she said, ignoring me. "Let's go."

"But I don't want to go to the cemetery tonight," Frog wailed. "I want to go to the party."

And then Sarah dropped a bomb.

"There'll be plenty of time for the party *after* we recover the money that was stolen from the Wilsonburg Bank."

□

18

"If you know where the stolen money is, you should tell Chief Radky," I told Sarah as we walked down Main Street.

"The Chief thinks I'm a pest," she reminded me. "But he'll change his mind when I tell him how we solved this case."

Frog and I tried pumping her for more information as we headed out Route 40, but she told us to be patient. When she turned from the highway on to the old abandoned road, we reluctantly followed.

There was nothing pretty about the woods at night, with only Sarah's flashlight to keep the dark-

□

ness from enveloping us. She led us to the black van and pointed her light at the license plate. As I remembered, it simply read D O G.

"I got to thinking about this license plate," she said. "If the owner is really a dog lover, it would read D O G S, not just D O G."

"What are you getting at it?" I demanded.

"Sometimes people use the initials of their name for their license plate identification. Since we had been talking about Doug Grimes, I began to wonder if maybe the D stood for Douglas and the G for Grimes?"

"That's why you wanted to know if Doug's middle name began with an O!"

"Exactly. And according to Goldie, it does."

Now I was looking at the license plate in a different way.

"If D O G stands for Douglas Oliver Grimes," I said, "then this is Doug's van! And I spotted it leaving the crime scene the night of the robbery!"

"Are you saying Doug robbed the Wilsonburg Bank, pretending to be the Village Bandit?" Frog gasped.

"Why not?" Sarah replied. "A lot of people seem to know that Paul Carmichael leaves the bank every Thursday night at eight o'clock for sandwiches. Why wouldn't Doug know it too?"

"But Chief Radky spoiled his plan," I added. "No

□

sooner did Doug drive away with the money than the Chief discovered Paul and Mr. Pennyman handcuffed in the bank."

"And Radky immediately called the State Police, requesting roadblocks around the county," Sarah said. "I called the State Police barracks this afternoon, and the desk sergeant told me that one of the roadblocks was set up on Route 40 *beyond* the cemetery."

"Doug must have been shocked to hear on the van's police scanner that the robbery had been discovered so soon," I reasoned. "With his reputation, he couldn't afford to even be *seen* at a roadblock after a major crime."

"And certainly not with bags of money, a ski mask, and a pistol in his van," Frog added.

"So he hid the van in here," Sarah replied. "And took off on foot with the money to find a safe place to hide it until he could come back when the coast was clear."

"So we've connected two dots!" Frog declared. "From the bank in town to the van in the woods."

"And now let's connect the third dot," Sarah finished. "I think I saw a path near here this morning."

She walked along the road, pointing her light into the woods, until she spotted a narrow path branching off in the direction of the cemetery. We fell in behind her in single file.

□

"I'll bet you anything Doug came this way with the money the night of the robbery," Sarah said over her shoulder.

The path twisted and turned and finally ended at an isolated section of the cemetery. We climbed the chain-link fence and dropped down on the other side.

"What now?" I asked.

"First, we stop at the caretaker's house," Sarah answered. "Then we go up on Cemetery Hill."

"This has something to do with that extra grave in the Wilson mausoleum, doesn't it?" I said.

"I'm counting on it," Sarah replied grimly.

19

WE WALKED ALONG the fence, which curved around
to the front gate. Randall was waiting for us on the
porch of the caretaker's house. He was wearing
long, flowing, old-fashioned clothes.

"I'm Galileo, the seventeenth-century astrono-
mer," he announced.

"Has your Mom left for the Community Center?"
Sarah asked.

"Yeah. She's meeting Paul there. I told her I had
to make some adjustments on my costume and I'd
come later."

☐

"Good. Do you have the key to the Wilson mausoleum?"

"Funny thing about that," Randall said as he handed Sarah a shiny new key. "The locksmith gave Mom two keys, but there was only one hanging on the peg in the office."

"I want you to go up to your observatory and watch the top of Cemetery Hill through your telescope," Sarah directed. "If you see Frog turn on that crazy spinning light on his head, it means we're in trouble. Call the police."

"It sounds like you're expecting trouble," Frog fretted.

"Not necessarily," Sarah explained. "But a good detective *always* has an emergency plan."

Randall ran into the house, and Frog and I followed Sarah up the road to Cemetery Hill.

"How do we even know the money is still here?" I asked as we walked through the pine grove. "How do we know Doug hasn't already come back and taken it?"

"The first time Doug returned to get the money, Randall scared him away," Sarah reasoned. "The second time he came, he ran into Mrs. Biddle in the Wilson mausoleum. It was a good thing for him he was wearing that mask or you and Frog would have identified him on the spot."

"And after that, Ms. Davis had that big new lock

□

put on the door," Frog added. "Not even Doug can break in."

"But why has he left his van in the woods?" I wondered.

"There are still a lot of unanswered questions in this mystery," Sarah admitted as we approached the Wilson mausoleum.

She then told Frog to hide in the bushes nearby.

"Don't take any chances," she warned him. "Signal for help if *anybody* comes around while we're in the mausoleum."

"I don't like this," I admitted.

"We won't be long," Sarah tried to reassure me as she unlocked the door and pushed it open.

I was shivering all over as we stepped inside. Maybe it was the cold, stale air. Maybe it was fear. Probably it was both.

Sarah turned her flashlight on.

"Find the panel that has the name 'Wallace Cornelius Wilson' on it," she said.

We began reading the marble panels that covered the graves stacked floor to ceiling in the three walls. The panel we were looking for was at the very bottom of the middle wall. It read:

WALLACE CORNELIUS WILSON
Born 1896 – Died 1916
He Gave His Life for His Country

□

"Now what's this all about?" I demanded.

"I asked Mrs. Esterly, the town historian, why there's one more grave in here than on the official cemetery record. She knows a lot about the history of the Wilson family."

"Go on," I said.

"She said that Wallace Cornelius Wilson was killed in France, fighting in World War One. He was buried *there*, not here."

"Then why is there a panel with his name on it?"

"Mrs. Esterly said Wallace's mother was so upset about his death that she insisted he be remembered in the family mausoleum, even though his body isn't here."

I crouched down and ran my hands over the panel.

"So, according to Mrs. Esterly, this grave is empty?"

"Right. Except *I* don't think it's *empty* empty. I think Doug stashed the stolen money in there after hiding his van in the woods."

Sarah reached for the panel.

"And now let's see if I'm right."

20

At each corner of the panel was a rose made out of brass. I watched as Sarah turned one around and around until she pulled it out. The roses were really long screws.

"I learned this from Mrs. Esterly," Sarah explained, as she unscrewed the others. "Pretty screws like these were used to hold the panels in place when the graves were empty. After a casket was placed inside, the panel was screwed back into the wall and permanently sealed shut with cement."

"That's why this panel was never sealed," I reasoned. "Because no body was ever buried in there."

□

Sarah grabbed the edges of the panel and pulled it slowly away from the wall. I helped her lower it to the floor. Then she pointed her light into the opening of the grave. Instead of a coffin, two canvas bags packed with money were sitting inside. A ski mask and small pistol lay on top of the bills in one of them.

"An empty grave in an old mausoleum," Sarah whistled as we pulled the bags out. "The perfect hiding place."

"But how did Doug know about this?" I wondered.

"Mrs. Esterly said that Oliver Grimes, the old caretaker, knew everything there was to know about the cemetery. At some point, Oliver must have told Doug the sad story of Wallace Cornelius Wilson and this empty grave."

"I guess Doug didn't have any trouble breaking in here the night of the bank robbery," I pointed out. "Ms. Davis said the old lock on the door was rusty and brittle."

"Let's get these bags down to the caretaker's house and call Chief Radky," Sarah said.

We each picked up a bag and turned toward the door, only to find the creature from the grave blocking our way. I was too scared to even cry out in terror!

And then I remembered there was no creature. It

was only a mask. That knowledge didn't stop my body from shaking. If Sarah was right, and Doug Grimes was behind the mask, we were in trouble big time. Doug is a violent person and now he had to know we were on to his crime.

From the neck down, he was dressed all in black. He was also gripping a huge flashlight like a club. He stepped forward and used it to motion us away from the money.

Just as our backs hit the wall, Frog switched on his emergency light to signal Randall. The swirling beam, cutting through the night outside, made it look like a police car was on the way. The intruder grabbed the bags of money and darted out the door.

"Come on!" Sarah cried. "We've got to keep him in sight for the police."

We followed him down the cemetery road, trying not to get too close. As we emerged from the pine grove he was running toward the locked front gate. I could see a car parked on the other side of the highway.

It looked like he was going to climb out and escape. But as he approached the gate, he suddenly skidded to a stop. As we got closer, I could see Mrs. Biddle and her Searchers for Psychic Truth were standing in a line on the other side. They had their eyes closed and were chanting something.

I figured our robber didn't want to get tangled up

□

with Mrs. Biddle and her friends, because he veered to the right and ran up to a section of fence farther down. There was no way he could climb out with the bags in his hands, so he heaved them over. Both landed on the other side and fell over, spilling money out on the ground. The bills were held together with paper bands, but one bunch broke open on impact. A wind picked up the loose bills and blew them down toward Mrs. Biddle and her friends.

"The wind may howl and the wind may lash, but the spirits are using it to send us cash!" Mrs. Biddle shrieked.

With cries of delight, the Searchers began running around trying to catch the swirling bills.

Seconds later, a police car screeched to a halt at the front gate. The robber was trying to stuff money back in the bags as Chief Radky and a deputy ran up to him.

"Chief!" Sarah called out. "Behind that mask is the man who robbed the Wilsonburg Bank!"

□

21

RADKY AND HIS DEPUTY quickly had the situation
under control. Sarah and I climbed over the fence
and joined them as Radky pulled off the mask. It
was the most shocking moment in a mystery filled
with shocks. The face blinking in the flashing lights
didn't belong to Doug Grimes.

"Paul!" I gasped. "Paul Carmichael!"

"I take it you expected someone else?" Radky said
when he saw our looks of complete confusion.

"*We* thought it was Doug Grimes," Sarah admitted.

□

"That would be a neat trick," Radky chuckled. "I know for a fact that Doug Grimes has been in jail in Pittsburgh since last Thursday night."

By then Randall had joined us.

"I called the police as soon as I saw Frog's light," he declared.

And then Mrs. Biddle and her friends gathered around.

"Beatrice," Radky said sternly. "I know you weren't actually *on* cemetery property tonight. But this is now a crime scene, so I want you to move along. No ghosts are going to appear after all this commotion anyway."

"You're right, Chief." Mrs. Biddle agreed. "Come, Searchers."

We watched as they disappeared down the highway, singing weird words to the tune of *Jingle Bells*:

"Halloween, Halloween, haunted all the way. Oh, what fun it is to search for ghosts at work or play. Hey!"

Radky then turned to Sarah.

"Talk to me!" he ordered.

Sarah was only too happy to oblige. By the time she finished our story, Radky was nodding his head in agreement.

"You weren't the only one who had trouble believing that the Village Bandit robbed our bank," he said. "My doubts were confirmed when the real

□

Bandit was arrested in Iowa. He confessed to every robbery he was accused of *except* ours."

"But I was wrong about Doug Grimes being the robber," Sarah pointed out sadly.

"Don't be too sure about that," Radky replied. "You've put together an impressive line of reasoning to implicate him. Don't give up so easily."

"But you said Doug has been in jail since the night of the robbery," Sarah reminded him.

"Yes, but he was arrested well *after* the holdup," Radky replied. "He got into a late night fight in a tavern in Pittsburgh and ended up assaulting a police officer. He had plenty of time to do what you're accusing him of doing here and then getting into trouble in Pittsburgh later."

Radky looked at Paul, who was staring grimly at the ground.

"If I know Doug Grimes, he'll be only too eager to talk when I confront him with all this," Radky said. "*And* he'll be more than happy to implicate someone else if he thinks it will help him bargain for a lighter sentence.

"Do yourself a favor, Paul. Beat him to it."

"OK, OK," Paul blurted out after Radky read him his legal rights. "Sarah is right about everything except what happened *after* Doug hid the money in the mausoleum."

"Go on," Radky urged.

□

"It was my idea to rob the bank and blame it on the Village Bandit," Paul confessed. "Doug was supposed to pretend to force me into the bank *after* I returned from the diner with the sandwiches. But that idiot did it *before*."

"Which led the Chief to come investigate," Sarah added.

"And that ruined everything!" Paul cried. "If Radky hadn't shown up and gotten roadblocks set up, Doug would have had plenty of time to drive the money back to Pittsburgh. We would have divided it up the next day."

Radky told the deputy to put Paul in the squad car.

"I'll question him further at the station," Radky said. "Then I'll go to Pittsburgh and talk with Doug. You kids go to the party, but meet me at the diner tomorrow."

"I bet Mom is wondering where Paul is," Randall said.

"Wait a minute!" I cried. "Where's Frog?"

We looked up the hill and saw Frog finally making his way down the road. The light was still spinning on his head.

"French fries!" he was yelling. "Get me some French fries!"

□

22

THE NEXT DAY Chief Radky met us for lunch before the football games. Ms. Davis and Mrs. Esterly, the town historian, were also at the table and, of course, everyone in the diner listened in.

"Our two *friends* talked their heads off last night," Radky grinned. "Sarah, I assume you'd like to now start the questioning?"

"Of course," Sarah began. "Paul said I had everything right except what happened *after* Doug stashed the money in the Wilson mausoleum. Where was I off?"

"You thought it was Doug Grimes lurking around

□

the cemetery in the monster mask," Radky explained. "You didn't know that Doug was stuck in jail, unable to make bail."

"So Paul Carmichael was behind the mask?" I said.

"Right. Doug called him from jail Friday morning and told him how the roadblock on Route 40 forced him to hide the van in the woods and stash the money in the Wilson mausoleum. He then snuck around the roadblock on foot, and hitchhiked back to Pittsburgh where he got himself arrested for fighting. Of course, Doug expected Paul to come right down and bail him out. Instead, Paul hung up the phone on him."

"A double cross!" Sarah cried. "Paul figured with Doug safely locked up in Pittsburgh, *he* would just go to the mausoleum and take all the money for himself!"

"Correct," Radky nodded. "Paul bought a mask to hide his identity and went up on Cemetery Hill Friday night."

"But he ran into me and my telescope," Randall declared.

"Yes," Radky chuckled. "So he ran away and came back the next night when he thought the coast was clear. But no sooner did he enter the Wilson mausoleum than he found himself mask to face with Beatrice Biddle. I have to give him credit though.

□

He pushed her down and knocked her out as he fled the scene, but he used the phone in his car to call for an ambulance."

"*Anonymously*, of course," Ms. Davis pointed out. "And then the next morning I had that big new lock put on the mausoleum door. Paul couldn't possibly get in without a key."

"I'm afraid that's why he asked you out," Radky went on. "When he picked you up, he was hoping for a moment alone, so he could slip into the office and steal the key."

"And he got his chance," Randall cried, snapping his fingers. "He was alone downstairs while we were all upstairs. That's why there was only *one* key to the Wilson mausoleum on the peg last night. Paul had taken the other one."

"This time Paul wanted to make *sure* he had the mausoleum to himself," Radky went on. "He knew Randall would be at the Halloween party. So he invited Ms. Davis to help him chaperon, so *no one* would be in the area."

"Do I know how to pick 'em or what?" Ms. Davis cried.

"Don't worry, honey," Mabel called out from the counter. "He had *me* fooled into thinking he was a great guy, too."

"Did Paul know the money was in an empty grave?" Sarah asked.

□

"No," Radky answered. "Doug just told him it was hidden in the mausoleum. That was all Paul figured he needed to know before ending the conversation."

"So if Sarah and Clark hadn't been in the mausoleum, he might not have found the money," Mrs. Esterly commented.

"I'm afraid Paul's plan to rob the bank and blame it on the Village Bandit was doomed every step of the way," Radky concluded.

Just then Mrs. Biddle came in and walked up to Sarah.

"Anytime you want to use my Ouija board again, just ask."

"Sarah used your Ouija board?" I asked in amazement.

"When she brought me the pie in the hospital, she asked my Ouiji board where the Village Bandit would strike next. And the board gave her the correct answer!"

"So that's why you didn't want to call the FBI and tip them off," I hooted. "Because you used a Ouija board!"

For the first time since I had known her, Sarah actually blushed. And that made us laugh even harder!

□

23

ON MONDAY EVENING the newspapers ran the full story of Paul Carmichael, Doug Grimes, and their crime. The *Pittsburgh Post-Gazette* put their photographs side-by-side on the front page. There was Doug, resembling a gangster, next to Paul, looking like . . . well . . . like a handsome bank teller.

"Such an odd couple," Mabel commented when she saw it. "How did they ever get teamed up?"

"They were in the same high school class," Sarah pointed out. "When Paul came up with the idea to

□

rob the bank and blame it on the Village Bandit, he knew Doug would want in."

The paper also printed an article by Mrs. Esterly telling the story of Wallace Cornelius Wilson and his heartbroken mother. Another article featured a photograph of Chief Radky congratulating Sarah for cracking the case. It went on to say that Radky had made Sarah an official deputy of the Wilsonburg Police Department.

"Do you think Chief Radky will ever regret making Sarah a deputy?" Frog asked me.

"You better believe he will!" I laughed.

Conrad Capshaw convinced the town council to drop trespassing charges against Mrs. Biddle. He also talked them into giving her and the Searchers access to the cemetery again. In return, Mrs. Biddle promised that she and her friends would help Ms. Davis in keeping the grounds tidy. She also promised there would be no weird psychic investigating if any visitors were in the cemetery.

The Saturday after Halloween was cloudy and chilly. Still, Frog and I decided to try and relax outdoors *without* Sarah. We avoided her and headed to our favorite hill overlooking the river. It's where we go when we want to count barges *and* be alone.

We sat on our favorite fallen log and stared silently at the river. Everything was quiet and peaceful.

□

"You know something, Clark?" Frog finally broke the silence. "This is boring."

"You're right," I grinned. "Let's go find Sarah."

□